HAPPY FEET™

MOVIE STORYBOOK

Copyright © 2006 Warner Bros. Entertainment Inc.
HAPPY FEET and all related characters and elements are
trademarks of and © Warner Bros. Entertainment Inc.

Published by Ladybird Books Ltd.
A Penguin Company
Penguin Books Ltd, 80 Strand, London, WC2R 0RL, UK
Penguin Books, Australia Ltd, Camberwell, Victoria, Australia
Penguin Books (NZ), 67 Apollo Drive, Mairangi Bay, Auckland, New Zealand.

ISBN-13: 978-18464-6200-9
ISBN-10: 1-8464-6200-2

PELUK 4962

10 9 8 7 6 5 4 3 2

LADYBIRD and the device of a ladybird are trademarks of
Ladybird Books Ltd.

Based on the film by George Miller

In the darkest depths of space spins a blue and green planet capped with ice and snow. If you travel towards the southern-most point of this globe, you will discover a remarkable nation of beings who sing from their hearts. They are the Emperor penguins, and the singing is their Heartsongs.

One penguin, Norma Jean, had a song so sweet that all the male penguins flocked to her, singing in the hope of becoming her match.

'Boys, boys!' she exclaimed. 'Give a chick a chance!'

Then a new song rang through the air. With a voice that would melt your heart, Memphis moved towards Norma Jean. She listened and then began her own song in tune with his. Their songs became love, and their love became the egg.

But all too soon, Memphis and Norma Jean had
to say goodbye. When the egg hatched, their baby
would be hungry. So in the tradition of the Emperor
penguins, all the mothers left to hunt for fish in the
deep waters far away, while the fathers remained to
care for their precious eggs.

'If only you could stay,' Memphis said sadly.

'There are no fish on the ice, my love,' replied
Norma Jean. 'You've got to stay here to do egg time.'
She passed the egg to him with the greatest of care,
and Memphis tucked it safely in his cosy brood pouch.

'Don't you worry about a thing, Norma Jean,' he
called after her. 'I'll keep it safe and warm till you
get back!'

Soon, the icy winds whooshed as another brutal winter descended. The father penguins huddled together with their eggs to keep warm.

'Share the cold . . .' Noah the Elder chanted.

'Warm thy egg!' the huddle replied.

A towering swirl glowed above the huddle, creating a vision of a Great Penguin giving forth fish.

'Give praise to the Great Guin who puts songs in our hearts and food in our bellies!' Noah's voice rang out.

But Memphis only had thoughts for Norma Jean.

'Oh, I think I wanna dance now!' he cried as he started shimmying and shaking to the memory of Norma Jean's Heartsong.

Then a terrible thing happened. The egg slipped out from his brood pouch and slid down into the freezing snow!

'Oh no! No!' cried Memphis. He raced to rescue the egg and found it half buried by the swirling snow. Quickly, he tucked it back into his pouch, glancing around to see if anyone was watching. 'No harm done. Everything's gonna be just fine,' he told himself, knowing deep in his heart that there is no greater mistake than for an Emperor penguin to drop his egg.

ay by day, the winter winds quieted and the bitter snows softened. At long last, the sun returned to the sky. Memphis's wait through the terrible winter was finally over.

CRACK! *Crack! Crack!* All across Emperor Land, the eggs began to hatch. Shouts of rejoicing rang across the ice as fathers saw their newborns for the first time. But Memphis stood alone, staring at his egg, waiting for a sign, a crack, a sound from within.

Nothing happened.

'I'm so sorry,' said his friend Maurice quietly.

Memphis closed his eyes, trying to shut out the memory of the dropped egg.

Maurice's newborn chick, Gloria, tapped the egg with her little beak. 'Is it empty?' she asked, nudging it again.

Tap-tap-tappity-tap.

And suddenly, the egg tapped back!

'Did you hear that?' Memphis exclaimed, relieved.

'Hey, I can hear you, little buddy. Pappy's here! *Whoaaaa*!' Memphis jumped back as one foot popped out of the egg, then another. The egg rocked and rolled until it flipped over. Two tiny feet landed on the ground and hippity-hopped over the ice.

'That's, uh, *different*,' Memphis said.

From inside the egg, muffled sounds could be heard. Gloria giggled. 'Come back, Mister Mumble!'

'Little Mumble – I like that!' Memphis said. 'Slow down there, little Mumble!'

But the egg was out of control! It careened up the slippery ice wall, then crashed onto the ground. *CRACK!* The egg shattered, and little Mumble was born.

'Come to Daddy!'

Baby Mumble hippity-hopped over the ice as fast as his little feet could carry him. The Emperor penguins had never seen anything like it.

'What're you doing, son?' Memphis asked nervously.

'I'm happy, Pa!' Mumble said.

'What're you doing with your feet?'

'They're happy, too!' exclaimed Mumble as he danced on the ice.

'I wouldn't do that around folks, son,' Memphis said. 'It ain't Penguin!'

Mumble stopped dancing. 'OK, Dad,' he said.

'Good boy. Now come here and get warm,' Memphis said. As Mumble charged into the cosy pouch under his father's belly, Memphis looked anxiously around. The other penguins had stopped staring at them – for now.

With the coming of spring, the penguin fathers and hatchlings eagerly waited for the mothers to return.

'What's keeping them?' asked Eggbert the Elder.

'I hope it's not a fish shortage,' replied Noah.

But in the crowd of waiting fathers, Memphis had his own concerns. He turned to Mumble. 'When you see your mama, no hippity-hopping, okay?'

'Sure, Pa!' Mumble said. 'But how will I know which one is my mama?'

'Oh, you'll know, all right,' Memphis said. 'She's got a wiggle in her walk, and a giggle in her talk, and a song so sweet it'll break your heart.'

'Wives-ho! Wives-ho!' a voice boomed across the land. The female penguins had returned!

Mumble raced across the ice to meet his mother. In his excitement, the little penguin forgot all about the promise he'd made to his father. He hippity-hopped as fast as his little feet could carry him.

'What's wrong with his feet?' exclaimed Norma Jean.

'Oh, uh – he'll grow out of it,' stammered Memphis.

'Mama!' cried Mumble.

'Oh, Memphis!' Norma Jean cried, cuddling her son. 'He's *gorgeous*!'

'Isn't he, though?' Memphis said with relief.

'Open up, sweetie,' Norma Jean said. 'Mama has a little something for you.' After she fed Mumble some of the small fish she had caught, Norma Jean looked at Memphis. 'It looks like we may be facing a lean season, Daddy.'

'Aw, honey, I'm not worried,' Memphis replied. 'As long as the three of us are together, everything's gonna be just fine.'

Surrounded by Memphis and Norma Jean's love, little Mumble grew. Soon he was big enough to start school at Penguin Elementary.

'Good morning, class,' Miss Viola said. 'Today we begin with the most important lesson you will ever learn. Does anyone know what that is?'

'It's our Heartsong, miss,' Gloria replied. 'The voice inside that tells you who you truly are.'

'Exactly, Gloria! Without our Heartsong, we can't be truly Penguin, can we?' asked Miss Viola.

'No!' all the chicks replied together.

'Now, let's all be very still. Take a moment – and let the voice you hear inside come to you,' Miss Viola encouraged the class.

'I'm ready!' Gloria piped up. She started to sing in a clear, beautiful voice. Mumble had never heard anything so lovely. All over Emperor Land, penguins stood still and listened.

'That was beautiful!' Mumble exclaimed.

'Mumble, why don't you share your Heartsong?' suggested Miss Viola.

'OK!' Mumble said. 'Mine's, um, *boom-boom-sssssshhhhh, chippita-chippita-whishhhhh! BOOM!*'

Miss Viola looked confused. 'You heard *that* in your heart?' she asked. 'My dear, that's not even a tune. It *should* sound like this: *la-la-la-la-la-la-laaah!*'

'OK,' Mumble said. He took a deep breath.

'LAAAA-*laaaa*-laaaaa-*LAAAAAA*-laaaaagggghhh!' His tuneless voice screeched over the ice, shattering the peace of Emperor Land.

All the chicks laughed at Mumble – except for one.

'Stop it! It's not funny!' Gloria said angrily.

'No. It's not funny in the least,' Miss Viola said.

'A penguin without a Heartsong . . . is hardly a penguin at all.'

Miss Viola called a meeting with Mumble's parents immediately.

'I've *never* heard anything like it . . .' she said sombrely. 'Did anything happen during early development?'

Memphis paused. The memory of dropping the egg came flooding back – but how could he admit what he'd done? Without thinking, he made another terrible mistake: He avoided the truth. 'No, it was a tough winter, I guess . . . and, uh, he did hatch a little late . . .' he muttered.

'To think my little Mumble might spend his life alone!' Norma Jean fretted. 'Never to meet his one true love–'

'Oh, please, Miss Viola,' Memphis said desperately. 'Isn't there anything we can do?'

Miss Viola paused. 'Well, there's always Mrs Astrakhan. If anyone can help, Mrs Astrakhan can!'

Mumble began private singing lessons with Mrs Astrakhan. His parents stood nearby, full of hope.

'Every little pengvin has a sonk in his heart!' Mrs Astrakhan declared. 'First, you must find a feelink. Happy feelink, sad feelink – *enormous* feelink. You feel it?'

Mumble listened deep within himself. 'I do!' he said excitedly.

'Good! Now let it out! Be spontaneous!'

Mumble closed his eyes. But instead of singing, his feet started to move, then tap – faster and faster! Soon his happy feet were flying across the ice, tapping out exquisite rhythms that spread joy through every inch of his body. Never in his life had Mumble felt such excitement. The song in his heart was finally free!

I did it! Mumble thought proudly. But when he turned around, Mumble saw something he didn't expect: Mrs Astrakhan banging her head in frustration.

'Disaster!' she cried. 'I never fail before! Never!'

Mumble was confused. How could dancing bring him such happiness but upset everyone else?

emphis stormed off. 'I told you I never
want to see that thing with the feet
ever again!' he shouted, wondering
deep down if all this was *his* fault.

'So what if he's a little different?' asked Norma
Jean. 'I like different!'

'He's not different!' Memphis exploded. 'He's
a regular Emperor penguin who's got to learn to
behave like one.'

But Mumble couldn't ignore the longing in his
heart. He had to dance again. So he found a place
far from the disapproving eyes. In the dazzling

freedom of dancing, Mumble was able to be
himself. He was so caught up in it that he didn't
notice a shadow passing overhead. Suddenly, a
menacing grin appeared in front of Mumble.

'Whatcha doin' there, flipper bird?' asked a big
brown skua bird. Three more mean-looking skuas
crowded eagerly behind him.

'Nothing,' Mumble said. 'What are you doing?'

'Just dropped in for a little lunch,' the skua
replied hungrily. 'Hmm . . . leg or wing?'

'What? No, not me!' Mumble exclaimed.

The big skua cackled and thrust Mumble to the ground, pinning the little penguin with his foot.

'Wait!' cried Mumble, hoping to distract him. 'What's that *thing* on your leg?'

The skua's eyes lit up as he showed off the yellow band on his leg. 'I got two words for ya: Alien Abduction!' he exclaimed. 'Dere's somethin' out dere – bigger than us, smarter, too, with flat, flabby faces and no beaks! Dey grabbed me and strapped me down . . . I blacked out. The next thing I knew, I woke up with this thing on my leg.'

'Did they try to eat you?' Mumble asked.

'Nope,' the skua replied. 'I guess my pitiful cries for mercy appealed to their better nature.'

'Can *I* appeal to your better nature?' Mumble pleaded.

'Nice try, kid,' said the skua. 'But . . . no!'

As the skua lunged forward, Mumble saw a way to escape. He jumped into a tight crevice between two ice ledges.

The skuas tried to peck at Mumble but couldn't reach him. Angry and hungry, they flew away, leaving Mumble shaken, alone and full of questions. Would he ever dare to dance again? And what about the Aliens – did they really exist? What strange worlds lay out there, far beyond the ice? Could one small penguin ever hope to know?

The days melted into weeks, and the young penguins shed their baby feathers as they became teenagers ready to graduate from school. But Mumble was still covered in fluff, and no matter how hard he tried, he could not sing. He spent his time in school daydreaming at the back of the class, and as a result, Noah the Elder refused to let him graduate.

'Who says my boy can't graduate?' Norma Jean asked indignantly. 'Let's have our own graduation ceremony!' She tossed bits of fluff into the air, though Memphis was all too aware that the watchful eyes of Noah and the other Elders were upon them.

Afterwards, Mumble hurried to catch up with the other graduates. They stood at the edge of the glacier, squabbling over who should jump into the water. No one wanted to be the first.

Except Mumble!

'What are you waiting for?' he cried as he dived into the shimmering water. Following his lead, the rest of the penguins jumped in, too. Mumble couldn't help but notice Gloria, who had grown into a sleek, beautiful penguin. He swam over to talk to her, but Gloria was distracted.

'FISH!' she yelled.

Hundreds of hungry penguins came from everywhere! There weren't nearly enough fish for them all, but Mumble managed to catch one.

'Gloria! Did you get any?' he asked.

She shrugged. 'Nope. Not this time.'

'Have mine!' he offered.

But just then, a hungry skua bird swooped down and grabbed Mumble's fish! The skua took off in flight, carrying both the fish and Mumble into the sky. Two more hungry skuas latched onto the fish and tried to fly even higher. Gloria swam beneath them, begging Mumble to let go.

But Mumble clung to the fish, determined to keep his prize. Exhausted by the struggle, the skuas finally let go of the fish. Mumble plummeted to the ice far below.

Gloria was soon by his side. 'Mumble?' she asked. 'Are you OK?'

'Take it,' he gasped, the battered fish still in his beak. 'It's for you.'

And in that moment, it was clear to Gloria that Mumble was truly special. 'Thank you,' she whispered as she reached down to accept the gift.

'You're welcome,' Mumble sighed.

That night, up on a tall iceberg, all the young penguins gathered together to celebrate their graduation. The brilliant lights of the Southern Aurora shimmered in the starry sky. Gloria sang a beautiful love song as the graduates swayed back and forth in harmony with her.

Mumble was so overcome by the beauty of her voice that he lifted his head to the sky and tried to sing along. *'AaaHHHHyeeeeeHEEEEEhaaaaahhhh!'* His screeching brought the concert to a sudden stop.

'What's *wrong* with you, Fuzzball?' a penguin yelled. 'You're spoiling it for everyone!'

Gloria's kind voice rose above the catcalls. 'Mumble,' she said gently, 'maybe you'd better just . . . you know . . . listen.'

'I know,' Mumble said heavily. He trudged away until he found a small ice pad. He could still hear Gloria's voice echoing across the water. *At least now I can enjoy her song . . . without ruining it for anyone else,* he thought before finally falling into a fitful sleep.

By morning, Mumble's ice pad had drifted far away. Suddenly, *wham*! A jolt woke him, then *snaaap*! The huge jaws of a leopard seal lunged at him, knocking him off the ice pad. Mumble swam as fast as he could, but the monster was too swift.

Snaaap! Its teeth closed around Mumble's tail. But Mumble wriggled free, losing only a few tail feathers. High above, Mumble saw his only chance to escape: a hole in the ice. He torpedoed through it and landed safely out of the predator's reach – right into five little penguins who were cheering wildly for him!

The Adelie penguins – Nestor, Rinaldo, Lombardo, Raul and Ramon – were small in size but big on attitude. They dared the Leopard seal to bite them – but the great creature, so terrifying in the water, was slow and clumsy on the ice. It soon gave

up, and Mumble danced for joy. *Tap-tap-tappity-tap!*

The Adelies were amazed. '*Amigo*, do that again!' urged one.

'This?' Mumble asked, showing off a few moves.

'Oh, yeah!' the Adelies yelled. 'You da bomb, bro!' As they turned to leave, Ramon called out,

'Ain't you coming, Tall Boy?'

Mumble looked out across the endless sea toward his distant home. 'Yeah. Why not?' he replied, and followed after them.

delie Land was like no place Mumble had ever imagined. Thousands of tiny Adelie penguins were everywhere – laughing, jumping and partying! Mumble towered above them all. He was different in both looks and attitude, but the Adelies didn't seem to mind. They liked him *because* he was different, and they even wanted to dance like him!

'With moves like that, you must have all the ladies drooling at your feet,' the Adelies said.

'I wouldn't say that,' Mumble replied shyly.

Ramon stopped him. 'Let me tell something to you. Except for me, Tall Boy, you got the most charisma of anybody!'

Mumble beamed. *That's the nicest thing anyone has ever said to me!* he thought, jumping into the Adelie conga line. The upbeat music and lively rhythms of Adelie Land came naturally to him. 'MAMBO!' they all yelled.

Soon, Mumble was adding new moves to the dance. The Adelies pushed him to the front of the line so that they could follow his lead. For the first time in his life, Mumble found himself surrounded by friends.

Just then, Mumble danced onto a thin ledge of ice. It cracked beneath his feet and he plunged straight down the side of a steep glacier. 'Whoo-hooooo!' he hollered.

'Man, this guy is so accidentally cool!' Nestor marvelled.

And one by one, the little penguins leapt after Mumble.

Down, down, down the penguins went, slipping and sliding and bumping off lumps of ice along the way. The lumps turned into larger chunks, until the snow and ice became an . . . *avalaaaanche*! Working as a team, the penguins managed to keep ahead of the landslide. They were thrown into the air and plunged into the sea.

The avalanche had freed something from the grip of the glacier – a massive metal creature called an excavator. The armour-plated creature, red in colour with big jaws, was unlike anything the penguins had ever seen before. It shuddered and groaned as it tumbled slowly, end over end, into the deep black waters below. As Mumble watched it fall, he thought, *Whatever it is, it doesn't belong here.*

'Guys! Hey, guys!' Mumble called out as he hurried to catch up with his friends back on land. 'What *was* that thing?!'

'How should we know? We're penguins,' answered the Adelies.

'You want answers?' Ramon asked. 'Then you got to see Lovelace!'

'Who's Lovelace?' Mumble asked.

'Lovelace is the Gooroo!' Nestor replied. 'He got the answer to everything!'

'But first,' added Ramon, 'you gonna need a pebble!'

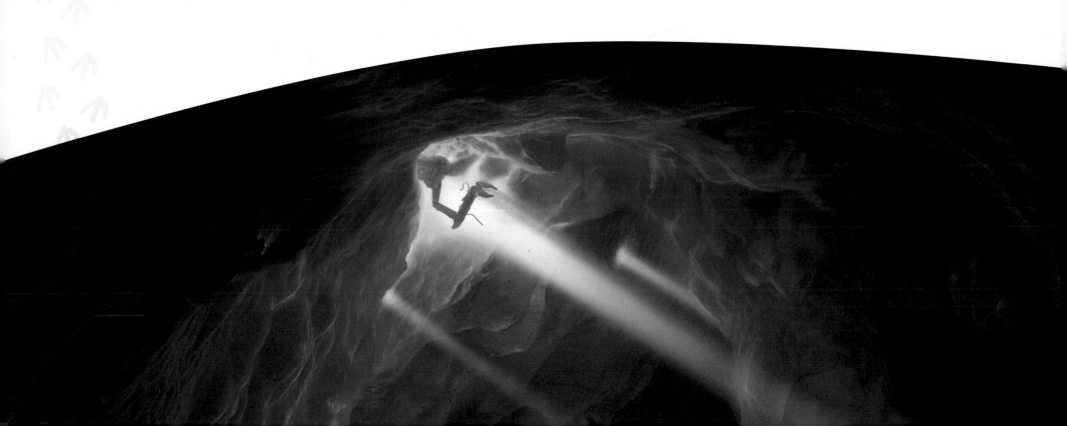

The Adelies led Mumble to a tall tower of pebbles, the world's biggest penguin nest. On top stood a Rockhopper penguin with flashy yellow feathers and gleaming red eyes. It was Lovelace himself – the all – knowing guru.

One by one, a long line of penguins offered him a pebble, hoping for answers to troubling questions. When it was Mumble's turn, he noticed something strange around Lovelace's neck: six connected rings. It reminded him of the plastic band wrapped around the skua's leg.

'Were you abducted by Aliens?' Mumble asked.

'*This* is my Sacred Talisman,' Lovelace said in a huff. 'It was bestowed upon me by the Mystic Beings during my Epic Journey of Enlightenment to the Forbidden Shore!'

'Did they have flat, flabby faces and no beaks?' asked Mumble. 'Did they grab you and strap you down?'

'One pebble, one question!' snapped Lovelace.

'But you haven't answered any of my questions!' protested Mumble.

'This stranger comes before me and *doubts my powers*?' Lovelace ranted. 'No more questions for today!'

With that, Lovelace waddled away behind his great pile of pebbles.

'It's not fair. He gets all the pebbles and all the girls,' Nestor complained.

'And we get nothing!' grumbled Rinaldo.

'Hey, Fluffy, you got any pebbles where you come from?' asked Ramon.

'We don't collect pebbles,' replied Mumble with a shrug.

'Then how do you win the heart of the ladies?' Rinaldo asked.

'We sing,' Mumble said.

'You kidding? That's crazy!' laughed the Adelies.

'If someone special likes your song, then . . . you know . . .' explained Mumble.

'Is there someone *especial* for you?' asked Rinaldo.

'Well, there would be,' sighed Mumble. 'If only I could sing.'

'You a bird, ain't you?' argued Raul. 'All birds can sing!'

I guess they'll only understand if they hear it for themselves, Mumble thought. 'LAAAAAA-laaaaaaa-laaaaaaa-LAAAAA!' It was the most painful screech in the world.

'Whoa – you in tragic shape, man. But don't worry. We can fix it!' promised Ramon.

'Really?' asked Mumble, his heart filling with hope. 'If I could *sing*, that would change everything!'

'Jus' do *exactly* what I say,' Ramon said.

Back in Emperor Land, the air was filled with Heartsongs. The lovely Gloria was surrounded by male penguins, all trying to woo her with their songs.

Suddenly, a new voice carried above the rest. As the voice serenaded her in Spanish, Gloria saw a familiar figure approaching her. Could it be . . . *Mumble*? But how had he learned to sing so well? And in Spanish?

Then she spotted little Ramon hiding behind Mumble's back, singing his heart out.

'Oh, Mumble!' she said. 'How could you fake your Heartsong?'

'Gloria,' Mumble pleaded as she turned away. 'I just didn't know what else to do!'

But Gloria kept walking, singing her Heartsong in a soft, disappointed voice.

'Gloria!' Mumble called desperately. 'Sing to this!'

Tip-tap-tippity-tappity-tippity-tap-tap!

His rhythmic tapping to her Heartsong was so intriguing that Gloria couldn't help but sing a few notes back. This moved Mumble to dance like never before . . . and his dancing ignited the love in Gloria's song. Together, her singing and his dancing became one, and the power of the music they made together was utterly infectious!

Soon, they were joined by all the other teenagers, singing and dancing together in perfect harmony.

It was the most brilliant moment of Mumble's life.

Suddenly, a shadow fell over Emperor Land. 'STOP! STOP! STOP THIS UNRULY NONSENSE!' thundered Noah the Elder, afraid that Happy Feet would infect the entire Emperor nation.

'But we're just having fun,' said the Adelies.

'Do you not understand that this kind of disorder will offend the Great Guin – and invite him to withhold his bounty?' asked Noah.

'Excuse me, Smiley,' interrupted Ramon. 'Can you speak plain Penguin, please?'

'He thinks Happy Feet is causing the food shortage,' Mumble answered.

'From the day you were hatched, there have been less fish,' said Noah. 'You and your silly hippity-hop . . . you were *always* a bad egg.'

'He speaks the truth, son.'

Mumble turned to see Memphis emerge from the crowd.

'If you give up your peculiar friends and your strange ways, the fish will return,' continued Memphis.

'But, Pa,' Mumble protested. 'It just doesn't make any sense.'

'Listen, boy, I was a backslider myself!' said Memphis, his voice heavy with regret. 'I was careless, and now you're all messed up.'

'Our son is not messed up!' Norma Jean exclaimed.

'I know that he is!' Memphis insisted.

Norma Jean was outraged. 'How can you say that?'

Before he knew it, Memphis blurted out these words: 'Because when he was just an egg . . . I dropped him!'

The crowd gasped. Finally Memphis had confessed his terrible secret.

'Oh, my poor little Mumble!' cried Norma Jean.

'But, Ma – I'm perfectly fine!' Mumble said.

'No, you're not, boy!' Memphis replied. 'For all our sakes, you must stop this freakishness with the feet.'

'Your father speaks wisely,' said Noah. 'You cannot be one of us if you cannot mend your ways.'

Memphis begged. 'Please, son. You can do it. It's not so hard.'

Mumble looked at his broken father and replied in a sad, quiet voice, 'Don't ask me to change, Pa . . . 'cause I can't.'

'And that, my brethren, is the end of it!' proclaimed Noah. 'You, Mumble Happy Feet, must go!'

Mumble was stunned. *How did this happen?* he wondered. He didn't fit in, but he never imagined he could be cast out . . . or that his own father would ask him to be untrue to himself.

He turned angrily to Noah. 'When I find out what's happening to the fish, I'll be back!'

The crowd parted to let him pass. And without looking back, Mumble and his five Amigos left Emperor Land.

Mumble was deep in thought as they wandered across the wasteland.

'He'll be OK,' Ramon reassured the others. 'All he's gotta do is find out what's happening to the fish.'

'How's he gonna do that?' asked Nestor.

'Aliens!' Mumble's eyes lit up. 'I'm going to talk to the Aliens. I bet they know what's going on.'

'How you gonna find Aliens?' Rinaldo asked.

'Lovelace!' said Mumble as he hippity-hopped towards Adelie Land.

They found the Guru slumped behind his great pile of pebbles.

'I have just one question,' Mumble said firmly. 'And I want a straight answer! Where do I find your Mystic Beings? These Aliens?'

Lovelace didn't answer. He couldn't. His big, booming voice was gone. He staggered towards them, gurgling and gasping.

'It's a seizure!' Rinaldo yelled.

'No, he's choking!' exclaimed Mumble. 'Those rings around his neck are too tight!' Through silent gestures Lovelace admitted the truth. The plastic rings were never bestowed on him . . . they had simply tangled around his neck while he was swimming along the forbidden shore.

'But this belongs to *someone*,' Mumble explained, pointing at the rings. 'And if we could find them, maybe they could take it off.'

Lovelace nodded with a glimmer of hope.
'Show me where you found it,' Mumble continued.
'I'm sure they could help us. You and me both.'

As Lovelace led them across the vast landscape, they heard a voice carried faintly on the wind.

'*Mumble!*' it called. '*Mumble Happy Feet!*'

It was Gloria . . . following them!

'What are you doing here?' Mumble asked, thrilled to see her again.

Gloria's eyes sparkled. 'I'm coming with you, Twinkle Toes.'

Mumble's heart sank. 'No,' he said. 'You have a life back there. We can't be together. Not out here.

How could we keep an egg safe?'

'I don't need an egg to be happy.' Gloria smiled back.

'You say that now,' Mumble countered. 'But what about later . . . when all your friends have eggs?'

'Then I'll have you,' she said simply.

With those words, Mumble's heart was filled at once with immense joy and desperation. He needed a plan to get her back to Emperor Land – and he knew what he had to do.

'You think you're irresistible, don't you?' he said, trying to sound detached. 'Just because you can hit a few high notes . . .'

'Excuse me?' said Gloria, shocked. 'Have you got a problem with my singing?'

This was the one thing Mumble knew would drive her back to Emperor Land. 'It's a little showy for my taste,' he shrugged. 'You know . . . flashy.'

The hurt in her eyes turned to anger. 'Showy? Flashy?' Gloria asked. 'That's outrageous coming from someone who thinks it's cool to jig up and down like a twitchy *idiot*!'

Mumble burst into a frenzy of dancing. 'What'd you say? I couldn't hear you over all the tapping!' he said loudly.

'*Argh!* You stubborn, hippity-hoppity fool!' Gloria turned her back on him and began the long walk home.

'That was a brave thing you did,' said the Adelies.

Mumble fought back tears as he watched Gloria go. 'Come on, guys,' he said. 'Let's keep going.'

The Land of the Elephant Seals was full of big, blubbery monsters, and the little band of penguins had to journey right through the middle of them.

'You fellas wouldn't be heading to the Forbidden Shore?' bellowed one of the giant seals.

The Adelies nodded, shaking with fear.

'Crikey. You might come face to face with an Annihilator,' said the seal.

'An *Alien* Annihilator?' asked Mumble.

'Cut you up as soon as look at you,' warned another. 'Annihilate everything living in their path.'

'Everything?' Ramon whimpered.

'Even if you're a whopping great whale,' groaned the formidable seal. 'They're merciless, mate, merciless.'

'Someone's got to stop them!' Mumble protested as he urged Lovelace and the Amigos forward.

'Oh, yeah? And what's gonna be your approach?' asked the seal sarcastically.

'If I could just talk to them . . . appeal to their better nature,' said Mumble, marching toward the darkening skyline.

'Your funeral, mate,' the biggest of the Elephant seals called after him.

With every passing mile, the winds grew more fierce, and Lovelace struggled harder for breath. They were in the Blizzard Country.

The penguins were blown backwards – until they found that by pushing together, they were able to withstand the terrible gale and keep moving onward into the night.

The following morning they found themselves in a place like no other: a strange Alien world littered with sharp hooks and rusty chains. Death hung in the air . . . this was the Forbidden Shore.

Lovelace led them past the bones of great whales to the water's edge. There, floating in all the junk, he pointed to plastic rings just like his. Then he collapsed, barely able to breathe.

'Hang in there, Lovelace!' Mumble said desperately. 'They must be here somewhere.'

With that, a great shadow loomed over them. But it wasn't the Aliens.

It was a killer whale leaping high out of the water and smashing down onto the ice . . . separating the penguins from the shore.

The whale was joined by another, and together they shoved the penguins, huddled on their ice pad, farther out to sea.

'Whatever you do, stay out of the water!' Mumble yelled.

But the plastic around Lovelace's neck caught on some junk as it slid off the ice. Lovelace was dragged down into the depths like an anchor.

To the Amigos' amazement, Mumble plunged in after him.

Try as he might, brave Mumble could not free Lovelace from the tangle of junk, and they both sank fast into the watery darkness.

The Adelies were certain they would never see their friends again . . . when suddenly one of the whales reared up out of the water with Mumble and Lovelace balanced on his snout! Like a skilled acrobat, he flung them high into the air, across to the other whale.

'What are they doing?' yelled Ramon.

'Playing with their food,' replied Nestor ominously.

The second whale tossed Lovelace and Mumble back to the first. As they cartwheeled through the air, Mumble heard a *snap*! The plastic had ripped from Lovelace's neck. He was free to speak again . . . but all he could do was scream as he flew like a tasty morsel toward the killer's gaping jaws.

Mumble reached out and grabbed Lovelace, who weighed him down. Together they plummeted into the water, just short of their surprised predator. They took advantage of the whale's confusion to

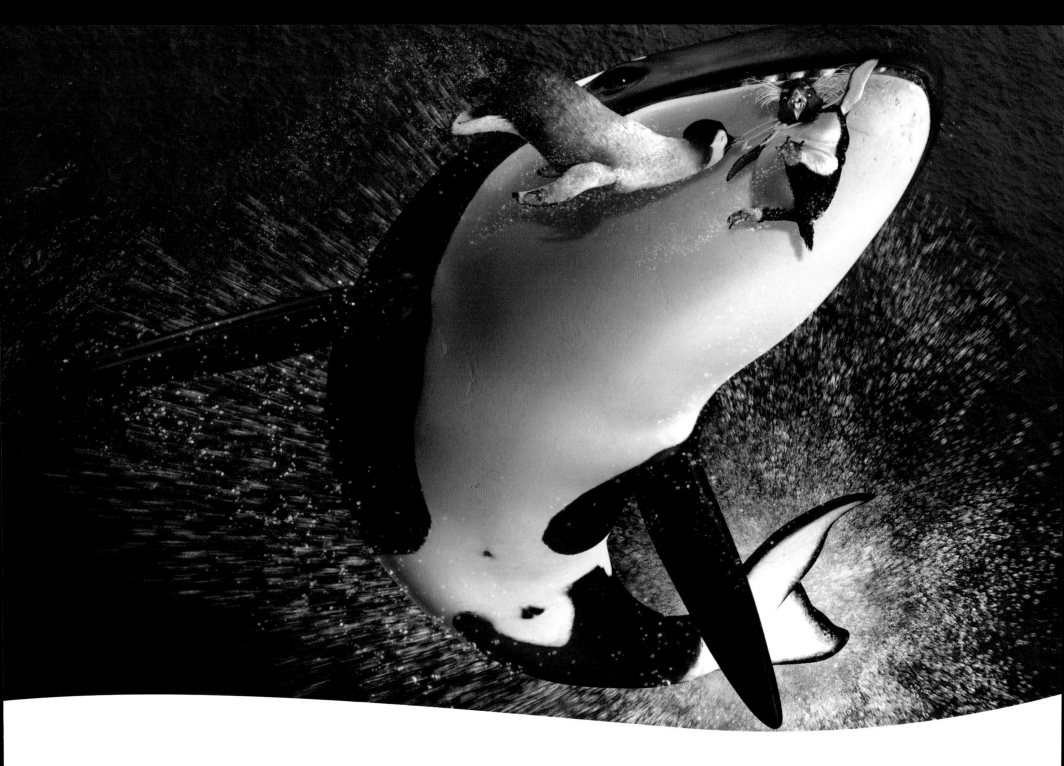

swim frantically to the shore, landing safely on the ice ahead of the lunging whales.

'ENOUGH!' Lovelace bellowed, making full use of his newfound voice. 'Begone, demon fish!'

To everyone's surprise, the whales turned and swam away in fear.

How did he do that? they all thought. *Amazing!*

Soon they knew the reason why . . . because right behind them came something bigger than an excavator, scarier than an Elephant seal, and more terrifying than a killer whale. A colossal black shape appeared out of the mist. The Alien ship sailed easily through the packed ice, which buckled and exploded as the ship passed, tossing the penguins back into the water. By the time they resurfaced, the Alien vessel was lost in the fog.

From the top of the tallest iceberg, they saw it again . . . it had joined other ships waiting on the horizon.

'They're gonna rule the world,' marvelled Rinaldo.

'What are they doing here?' asked Mumble.

'Let me tell something to you,' Ramon said firmly. 'This is the end of the road. You did everything penguinly possible.'

'You found the Aliens,' agreed Lombardo.

'We gonna tell your whole laughing-boy nation that they were dead wrong about you!' said Raul.

'Now let's all go back home!' Nestor finished.

But Mumble could not turn back now. 'Would you do me a favour?' he asked his friends. 'Would you make sure Gloria's OK? And my ma. And tell Pa . . . I tried.'

'What are you talkin' about?' said Raul. Mumble's words frightened them.

'I'm going to find out what's happening to our fish!' As he dived off the edge of the tallest iceberg, Mumble yelled, 'Adios, *amigos*!' And as he sailed through the air, towards the water far below, a curious thing happened . . . all of his baby feathers came off his face and body.

When he finally surfaced, Mumble was fluffy no more.

As he swam resolutely towards the ships, it occurred to his friends that they might never see him again.

Lovelace called out to him, making this promise: 'Wherever I go, I'm gonna be tellin' your story, Happy Feet, long after you're gone.'

But Mumble did not hear his friend. He swam with one goal in mind: to solve the riddle of the fish. He did not expect to have his answer so soon.

A sudden turmoil in the water caught his eye. A huge net rose slowly from the depths, and it was brimming with fish! Enough fish to feed whole nations of penguins. The Aliens were plundering the seas!

'Wait!' Mumble yelled. 'Stop!' He grabbed onto the bulging net with his beak and was lifted out of the water. But a penguin so small was no match for the Aliens. They poked him with long poles and he fell back into the sea, where massive propellers sucked him under and spat him out.

When he finally surfaced, the ships were on their way.

An ordinary penguin would have quit right there and gone back to his friends and family and told them what he had discovered. But not Mumble.

Enraged by the indifference of the Aliens, he followed the ships long after they were gone from his sight. He swam farther than any penguin had gone before . . . beyond all hope of return.

Swept up in great currents, he was carried endlessly across vast oceans to worlds unknown. One after another, the waves pushed him down.

Mumble gasped for air and tried to swim just a little farther . . . darkness swirled around him . . . against his will, Mumble submitted to the ferocity of the

water. He couldn't see; he couldn't swim; he could breathe no more. Unconscious, Mumble was carried to the shore by the waves.

Among the rubbish and the waste and slippery pools of spilt oil lay a motionless creature: Mumble Happy Feet.

Mumble would not remember the flashing headlights, the roar of the truck, or the gentle hands that lifted him off the polluted shore. But he did remember walking down the dark tunnel toward the blinding light. He arrived in a place that looked a lot like his homeland in Antarctica. There were lots of penguins, there was snow, and there were distant icebergs. But something was not quite right.

'What is this place?' Mumble asked a penguin who was feeding from a bucket full of fish.

'You're in heaven, friend. Penguin heaven,' the stranger replied in a zombie-like voice.

'Is it anywhere near Emperor Land?' asked Mumble.

'It's wherever you want it to be,' said the zombie penguin.

Mumble started walking towards the horizon. *Bang!* He had walked into a painted wall! The snow, the ice – almost everything around him was fake.

'Try the water,' suggested the zombie penguin. 'It's really real.'

Mumble dove into the water, swam a few strokes, and again, *bang*! He bumped into a glass wall.

And there, staring at him from behind the glass, were two Aliens up close! They were just as the skua had described, with flat, flabby faces and no beaks.

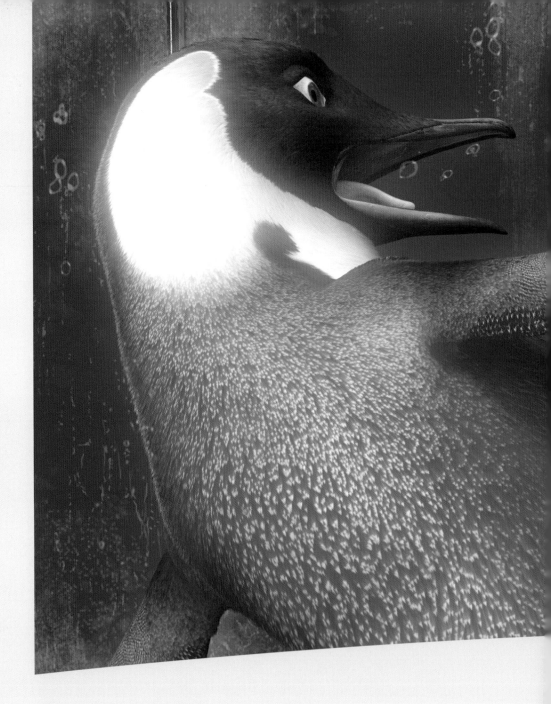

Then he noticed dozens more Aliens.

Overcoming his shock, Mumble pleaded with them, 'Why are you taking our fish? I'm sure you don't mean to, but you're causing an awful lot of grief.'

The Aliens did not respond.

'Am I not making myself clear?' Mumble shouted. 'I'm speaking plain Penguin!'

The Aliens still did not respond.

'Please! Doesn't anyone speak Penguin? YOU'RE STEALING OUR F-I-S-H!' Mumble yelled at the top of his voice.

But how could Aliens understand a squawking penguin trapped in a zoo? Here in this artificial world, where he was perfectly safe and had all the fish he could eat, Mumble lost all track of time – and all sense of who he was.

And his story would have ended there if it had not been for . . .

Tap. Tap. Tap.

A little human was tapping on the glass to get his attention.

Tap. Tap. Tippity-tap.

Something in Mumble, a small memory, awoke.

Almost involuntarily, his feet began to move.

Tap-tap-tippity-tap.

The little girl laughed.

Tap-tap-tippity-tappity-tippity-tap-tap! A half-remembered rhythm swelled in Mumble's heart as he began to dance.

Although it was closing time at the zoo, humans began to gather. The more he danced, the more the Aliens laughed and clapped and beamed with delight. Mumble had finally found a way to reach them!

'He's communicating with us,' a man said. 'We tap – he answers!'

'Where on earth did you find this creature?' asked another man.

'He washed up on a beach,' the zoo keeper replied.

'How did he get there?'

'Who knows? Swam all the way from Antarctica!'

'Amazing!' said the crowd.

Back in Emperor Land, things were a lot worse. The shortage of fish had broken the spirit of the Penguin nation.

Then one day, a voice rang out across the ice.

'Hello! Everybody, listen up! I've got big news!'

The listless crowd was surprised by the sleek, well-fed penguin approaching them.

'Hey, isn't that the guy with the wacky feet?' someone asked.

'I know who's taking the fish!' Mumble called out. 'It's the Aliens! I made contact with them!'

'Yeah, right! The lunatic is back,' was the skeptical response.

'*Mumble Happy Feet?* Is that you?' A lovely penguin came forward.

'Gloria!' exclaimed Mumble, his heart leaping at the sight of her.

Then he noticed many baby penguins gathered at her feet. *It's too late,* he thought, crushed by the realization that she was taken. 'So – which one's yours?' he asked, trying to hide his disappointment.

'All of them,' Gloria replied. 'This is my singing class.'

'So you never met your –' Mumble began.

'I never heard the right song, I guess,' said Gloria.

'Oh!' Mumble's eyes lit up with relief. He had so much to tell her. 'Oh, Gloria. The Aliens! They're big and kind of ugly – but they can do amazing things, and they're coming here! They want to help us!'

'So you talk with them?' Gloria said doubtfully.

'Not exactly . . . but they seem to respond to this . . .' *Tap-tap-tappity-tappity-tap!* he said with his feet. 'It appeals to their better nature.'

The crowd sniggered. *How ridiculous!*

Then Noah and the other Elders arrived. 'SO! You dare to come back!'

'He says he's found Aliens, and they're taking our fish!' a young penguin called out.

'THERE IS NO SUCH THING AS ALIENS!' Noah thundered.

And that's when they heard the unfamiliar sound.
Beep! Beep! Beep!

There, stuck to Mumble's back, was a *computer chip* with a flashing red light and tall antenna.

'Does it hurt?' asked Gloria.

'No,' Mumble said. 'It belongs to the Aliens. I think it's a way for them to find me, that's all.'

'You led them here?' cried Noah, outraged. 'You turned them on your own kind?'

'You just said there's no such thing as Aliens,' Gloria argued in Mumble's defense.

'But if there were . . .' stammered Noah, 'only a traitor would bring them here.'

The crowd was becoming more confused and agitated.

'But they have to come!' Mumble assured them. 'They're the ones causing the problem! They can do something about it!'

Gloria nodded in agreement, as did many others.

'Beware,' Noah commanded. 'A fool returns this day to mock our suffering. We are starving, and he wants us to *hippity-hop*!'

The crowd was divided.

Beep! Beep! Beepety-beep! The red light began to flash faster, and the sound became louder.

And that was enough for one young penguin. 'Hey, Mumble!' he cried out. 'Teach me how to *happy feet*.'

Mumble showed him a few steps.

Soon they were joined by others, until half the crowd began to tap to Mumble's catchy rhythms . . . while the other half took Noah's lead and began to *chant*.

'My baby boy is back!' shouted Norma Jean as she pushed through the crowd, followed by the Amigos. When Mumble had given each of them a great big hug, he looked up to see the forlorn figure of his father.

'Son? Is it truly you?' said Memphis, overcome with emotion.

'Every last bit of me, Pa,' Mumble replied softly.

'Dance for him, Daddy!' urged Norma Jean. 'Dance for your boy.'

'You have to forgive me,' sighed Memphis. 'The music's gone clean out of me.'

'No, it hasn't!' insisted Mumble. 'It's just one big old foot after another!'

Memphis wasn't sure where to start, but he followed Mumble's lead. As he moved his feet, the joy flowed up through his body and into his heart.

As he chanted loudly, Noah saw that the bond between the father and the son had been restored.

Just when the dancing and the chanting and the beeping had reached a crescendo, there came a sound that drowned out all the others.

Whoosh-whoosh-whump-whumpputy-whump. The Aliens had arrived.

Their huge helicopter landed, and five humans clambered out. They looked across Emperor Land and saw thousands of penguins staring at them in amazement.

For a long time, not one creature moved – neither human nor penguin.

Then Memphis turned to Mumble. 'I think you'd better dance now!' he said.

Mumble began to dance a simple rhythm, and one by one, others joined in: his father, his mother, his sweetheart, Gloria, and his true Amigos.

Then ten more penguins, then a hundred, then a thousand, then tens of thousands . . . even Noah and the other Elders – the whole community was dancing for the humans!

And a most extraordinary thing happened . . . the humans danced back.

The penguins, of course, would never know that the humans were scientists or that the scientists would present the amazing story of the dancing penguins to a congress of nations.

And they would never know that the international congress would go to great lengths to make laws to protect them, their home, and their food supply.

But when the fish came back and their waters were rich with life once more, the penguins *did* know that Mumble was somehow responsible for saving them all.

And if you visit that snow-covered land, you will find them . . . with the songs of their hearts and the rhythms of their dance merging in a glorious harmony.

You might even see Mumble and Gloria together, as they were always meant to be.

And if you listen very carefully, amid all the celebrations, you will hear the penguins calling out the name of the one who was brave enough to be truly himself, no matter where it would lead.

'MUMBLE *HAPPY FEET*!'